Dear Parent:
Your child's love of reading starts here!

Every child learns to read in a different way and at his or her own speed. Some go back and forth between reading levels and read favorite books again and again. Others read through each level in order. You can help your young reader improve and become more confident by encouraging his or her own interests and abilities. From books your child reads with you to the first books he or she reads alone, there are I Can Read Books for every stage of reading:

SHARED READING
Basic language, word repetition, and whimsical illustrations, ideal for sharing with your emergent reader

BEGINNING READING
Short sentences, familiar words, and simple concepts for children eager to read on their own

READING WITH HELP
Engaging stories, longer sentences, and language play for developing readers

READING ALONE
Complex plots, challenging vocabulary, and high-interest topics for the independent reader

ADVANCED READING
Short paragraphs, chapters, and exciting themes for the perfect bridge to chapter books

I Can Read Books have introduced children to the joy of reading since 1957. Featuring award-winning authors and illustrators and a fabulous cast of beloved characters, I Can Read Books set the standard for beginning readers.

A lifetime of discovery begins with the magical words **"I Can Read!"**

Visit www.icanread.com for information on enriching your child's reading experience.

To Carla and her wonderful
mother, Nadine Topalian
—J.O'C.

For Lisa Becker, with luck
and love
—R.P.G.

For M60S, the human four-
leaf clover: rare and a
magnet for good fortune
—T.E.

I Can Read Book® is an imprint of HarperCollins Publishers.

ISBN 978-0-06-208314-2 (trade bdg.)—ISBN 978-0-06-208313-5 (pbk.)

13 14 15 16 17   LP/WOR   10 9 8 7 6 5 4 3 2 1   ❖   First Edition

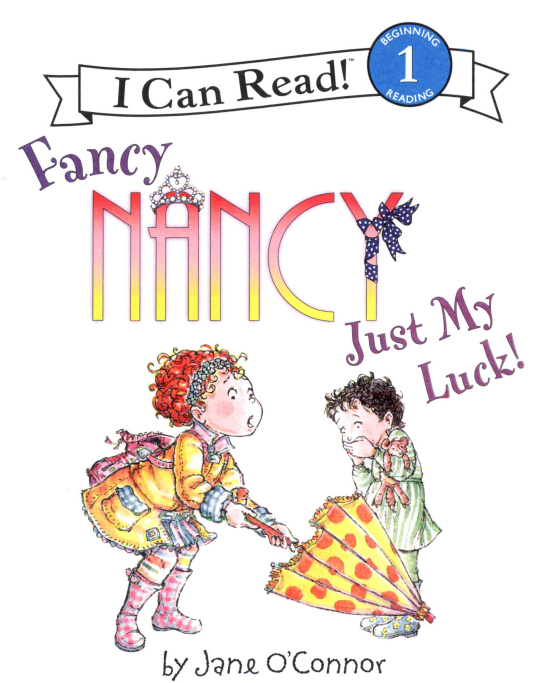

I Can Read!

BEGINNING READING 1

Fancy NANCY

Just My Luck!

by Jane O'Connor

cover illustration by Robin Preiss Glasser

interior illustrations by Ted Enik

HARPER

An Imprint of HarperCollinsPublishers

For show-and-share,

Clara has a four-leaf clover.

She passes it around.

5

"Four-leaf clovers bring good luck,"
Clara tells everyone.

"They bring even more good luck
than finding a penny."

Ms. Glass isn't positive that is true.
(Positive is fancy for
sure about something.)
She says, "I don't believe
in good-luck charms.
But four-leaf clovers are quite rare.
There aren't a lot of them.
So Clara is lucky to have one."

At recess, I decide to find

a four-leaf clover of my own.

Lionel helps.

Here is what we find:

a key and some string,

a wheel from a toy car,

and Robert's library card.

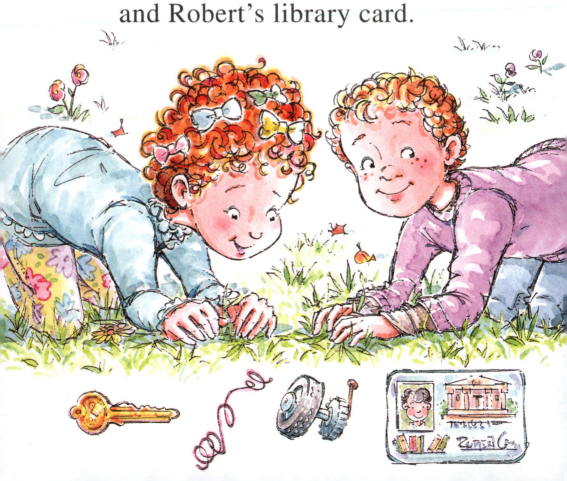

"Thanks!" Robert says.

He puts the card in his pocket.

It is hard because

he is upside down.

"I'm lucky you found it."

On the way inside,

I hear someone shouting.

It is Grace from the other class.

"Didn't you see what you just did?

You stepped on a crack," Grace says.

She points to a sidewalk square.

There is a big crack in it.

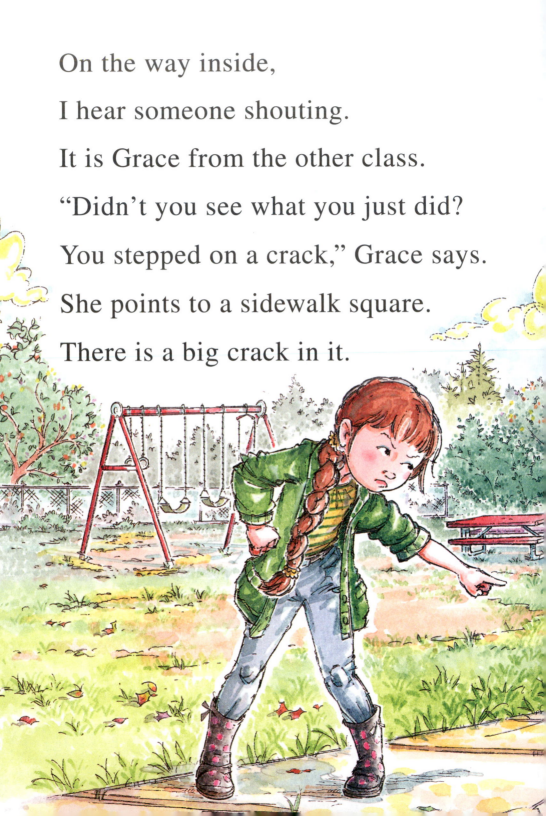

"So what?" I say.

"Duh!" says Grace.

"Don't you know that's bad luck?"

"No," I say.

"I was not aware of that."

It turns out that

Grace is an expert on bad luck.

(Expert is fancy for

someone who knows a lot.)

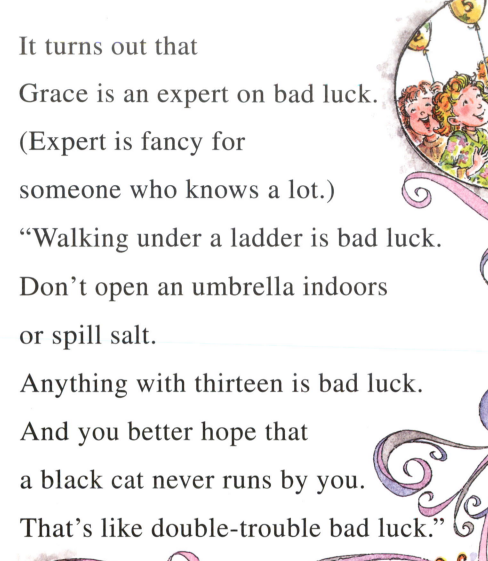

"Walking under a ladder is bad luck.

Don't open an umbrella indoors

or spill salt.

Anything with thirteen is bad luck.

And you better hope that

a black cat never runs by you.

That's like double-trouble bad luck."

Wow!

There are so many bad luck things

to keep track of!

13

At lunch,

I spill pudding on myself.

Maybe it's because I stepped

on the sidewalk crack.

For bad luck, it is not so bad.

But from now on,

I need to be more careful.

On the way home,

I try not to walk on any cracks.

I have to back up

and leap over this one.

Whew! I just made it.

At home,

I check all the mirrors.

Whew! None of them have cracks.

At dinner,

JoJo bangs my arm by accident.

I almost spill some salt!

Whew! That was a close call.

16

The next morning it is raining.

I almost forget about

not opening an umbrella inside.

Whew! That was another close call.

All day I stay away from thirteens.

I eat fourteen veggie chips.

I use twelve pipe cleaners.

Then math gets me in trouble.

One of the problems

is six plus seven.

When Ms. Glass calls on me,

I say, "Thirty-seven?"

I know that is incorrect.

(That is fancy for

wrong, wrong, wrong!)

But maybe saying "thirteen"

will bring bad luck—big, bad luck.

By the end of the day,

I am exhausted—

that is way more tired than tired.

"What's wrong?" Ms. Glass asks.

"I knew the answer

was thirteen," I say.

I explain about bad luck stuff.

"Keeping bad luck away

is hard work!"

Ms. Glass puts an arm around me.
"Nancy, don't worry about
any of these things.
They aren't true. I promise."

I want to believe Ms. Glass.

Ms. Glass is very wise, after all.

(That is fancy for extra smart.)

Walking home,

I try not to think about cracks.

Then, a block from my house,

something terrible happens.

A black kitten comes out of nowhere

and runs across the sidewalk.

Grace says a black cat

is double-trouble bad luck!

A second later,

a boy turns the corner.

"My kitten got out of the house!

Have you seen it?"

"The kitten went into the park!"

I tell the boy.

Without thinking,
I help him look.
It's just a lost kitten
that needs my help.

At last, I spot the kitten.

It is in the playground tube.

I block one end of the tube.

The boy crawls in . . .

and out he comes with his kitten!

"Thanks so much!" he says.

"It sure was good luck

that you saw where she ran."

Seeing a black cat

wasn't bad luck at all!

Grace is mistaken.

Ms. Glass is correct.

Just before I get home,
I see something shiny
in a puddle.
It is a penny—a new penny.
Maybe it will not bring
good fortune.

I put it in my pocket anyway.

After all,

if I find ninety-nine more,

I will have a dollar.

And that *is* almost a fortune!

Fancy Nancy's Fancy Words

These are the fancy words in this book:

Exhausted—way more tired than tired

Expert—someone who knows a lot

Incorrect—wrong, wrong, wrong!

Positive—sure about something

Rare—not a lot

Wise—extra smart